This book belongs to:

....

Anna Gets Her Wish
LesAnn Scott • Karen Edden

"I can't come up with just one wish! I can think of a gazillion." But Chrystabel had said just one wish. She had to think.

Lying in her cosy bed that night, under her soft eiderdown, her mind had gone wild with ideas until it came to her. She knew just what she wanted … and then she fell soundly asleep.

Bright sunshine was what she was hoping to wake up to the next morning. But no such luck. It had rained **ALL** night!

"Oh no! It's raining." Anna peeped through her bedroom curtains at the mass of grey clouds that looked like they were setting in for the day.

She had to get to Chrystabel or she would lose her wish and she had thought so long and hard about it.

Chores came first anyway ... if Gram would even let her go outside to do them. Anna was determined to try.

Maybe if it wasn't too heavy, Gram might let her go out with her wellies and her brolly.

Bright blue wellies with little yellow ducks stood near the front door.

Anna pulled them on over her fluffy pink socks. Then she buttoned her mackintosh and pulled the hood over her head.

Now, all she had to do was convince her Gram to let her go.

She grabbed the egg basket and went to tell Gram she was off to get some eggs.

Frowning, Gram looked out through the blue and white checked curtains to the yard outside. You could see she was thinking about it.

"Go quickly Anna, it's starting to let up a bit."

Without any hesitation, and before Gram could change her mind, Anna was off to do the chicken run.

Drat! All the chickens were inside (understandably with the weather) and Anna knew Mrs Chooks was going to peck her to pieces as she retrieved the eggs.

Then she had a brainwave, pulled her woollen mittens from her pockets to protect her hands and went from hen to hen pulling out the eggs. Strange thought Anna, that's five less than usual.

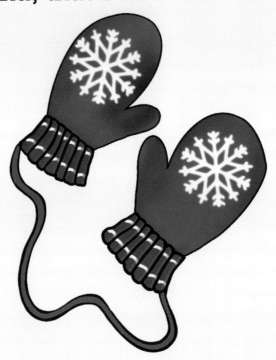

She then filled the inside feeders for the hens with grain and made a hasty escape.

No time to visit the Piggly Wigglys today.

She had something *very* important to do.

Breakfast was ready when she got back. The smell of bacon wafted through the kitchen.

"Gram, we were five eggs short today. Do you think someone pinched them? I looked carefully under each hen."

"That's very strange. I don't think so Anna but I will let Gramps know."

Anna plonked herself down on the wooden bench as Gram placed bacon, fried eggs and toast in front of her. "What are you going to do today Anna?" enquired Gram. "I am going to do some baking for the church fete if you want to help."

"I was hoping to visit my little house this morning and see if it's all okay after the rain. Please may I Gram?"

"Sure sweetheart, maybe you should go now while it's just a light drizzle. Stay warm please. Then perhaps you can help when you get back."

Anna jumped up and gave Gram a big hug.

She didn't need to be told twice and almost gobbled down her breakfast so she could finish quickly.

She grabbed her wellies and mackintosh again and hurried up the path happily jumping in all the puddles along the way.

She hadn't felt this happy in a long time. Mommy and Daddy weren't forgotten but somehow the heartache of losing them didn't feel so bad today.

Everything looked fine at the house. She wasn't quite sure what to do when she arrived so she tapped on the little door.

KNOCK KNOCK KNOCK!

She waited for Chrystabel. Nothing. She tapped again.

KNOCK KNOCK KNOCK!

Still nothing…

Opening the door, she peeked inside. There was no one there. Did she imagine all this?

The wind rustled through the trees and suddenly a little robin redbreast flew in and landed by the house.

There on his back were three little flower fairies.

One of them had a little green leafy cap covering her hair and a cape made from yellow tulip petals covered her wings.

The other one was a boy!

Do you get boy fairies?
It seems that you do,
thought Anna.
Well, that was a surprise.

And then she saw Chrystabel.

"We needed a bit of help this morning, after all that rain" explained Chrystabel.

"Robin came to the rescue. He flew us to the place where we last saw the missing fairies. Robin also knows just where to find our favourite berries."

Turning to the other two fairies she
introduced them,
"This is Lilyann and this is Zip."

"Sparkle should be arriving
shortly. She is still busy
looking for others
in the forest."

"Hi," Anna said shyly.

Lilyann smiled back and waved. She wore a little yellow skirt made with lily petals of course.

Zip wore green from head to toe.

Anna couldn't stop staring at him. He even had those little shoes with pointed toes like you see in story books.

She wondered if he was called Zip because he moved so fast.

She did notice that Zip stared at her as well and it wasn't pleasant.

He had an angry look on his face. What was that all about?

Chrystabel moved towards Anna and the other two took hold of the sacks they had been carrying which were still sitting on Robin's back. They grabbed them and carried them into the tree house.

Robin took off into the air whistling something as he flew off.

"Goodness me, we were so hungry.

We had to go and find some food out in the forest.

And we have to keep our eyes out for all our missing friends," sighed Chrystabel.

But tell me Anna," wondered Chrystabel, "have you decided on your wish?"

 This was Anna's big moment.

"I have," said Anna timidly.

"Maybe you will think it's silly. One day when I grow up I want to be a vet like my friend Sara's daddy and look after all the animals.

I want to be able to talk to the animals so that I can really help them.

May I wish for that?" queried Anna.

"Of course you may. Are you sure Anna? I only have one wish for you."

Anna nodded her head.

"Then let's do it," said Chrystabel.

Out of nowhere, it seemed, Chrystabel suddenly had a wand in her hand. She flew up towards Anna and tapped her on the top of her head.

As she did that, Anna noticed that the wand glowed and so did the little crown on Chrystabel's head."

"You have a crown!" exclaimed Anna.

"Are you a Fairy Queen?"

"No." said Chrystabel. "I am just a princess. My mother is the Queen. Until my mother is found, I have to wear the crown.

That's why I could give you your wish. Only the Fairy Queen can give a wish. And now you have your wish. I am so happy for you Anna."

"I do?" yelled Anna.

"Really? I don't feel any different."

"Time to go and test out that wish Special Anna. See you later." And with that Chrystabel stretched her wings and flew off.

Immediately, Anna set off at a run, straight to the farm yard. She just couldn't contain her excitement.

First she arrived at the chickens. Perhaps she could explain to Mrs Chooks why she had to take her eggs and she could find out about the missing eggs.

"Hello Mrs Chooks."

An angry Mrs Chooks clucked furiously.

"I don't suppose you could tell me why we were short of eggs this morning?"

Lots more clucking and squawking was the only response.

Well that didn't seem to work.

Wasn't she supposed to talk back?

Anna walked towards the Piggly Wigglys.

"Hello Mr and Mrs Piggly Wiggly, how are you today? Did you enjoy the rain? Do you have any idea why we are short of eggs today? Do we have a thief in the farmyard?"

They grunted and snuffled – more than usual - and then just pushed their snouts into their mash.

Bewildered, Anna decided the spell must not be working. Perhaps it was because Chrystabel wasn't the queen – she was just a princess.

Oh well!

A disappointed Anna walked off, kicking up dirt with the heel of her boots as she walked.

Whilst she was in the farmyard she decided she would do a bit of detective work and have a look around the chicken coop for footprints.

Other than her own wellies she could only see a few small footprints that looked like they might belong to Mr Fluffles, the grumpy farm cat. But he wouldn't steal eggs.

Perhaps the rain had washed away the evidence.

She made her way over to the big red barn and spotted old Hank the ancient carthorse. She stroked his mane.

"I don't suppose you know who stole the eggs?" Hank looked at her with big concerned, doleful eyes.

Anna imagined if he could talk right now, he would probably sound like Eeyore, Winnie the Pooh's gloomy grey donkey. The thought of that made her giggle a bit.

"Sorry Old Hank, I just feel so disappointed today. I don't even have an apple for you." Anna reached into her pockets to see what was in them. Just an old sweetie paper. No apples.

"Not to worry," replied Hank, "maybe next time."

He talked! Anna nearly fell over in shock. It worked, it really had worked.

She jumped up and down with excitement. She grabbed Hank's mane. "You talked, you talked."

And guess what, now she couldn't even tell anyone because it was a **HUGE** secret.

Why did secrets have to be like that?

"Yay Hank! It worked. Now maybe you can tell who stole the eggs." In her excitement she twirled around and did a little dance.

As she turned around she saw her friend Sara standing near the barn with a shocked look on her face.

Oh dear! Oh no!

This was supposed to be a secret.

Had Sara seen and heard **everything**?